MW01491234

Bench Therapy

Book One

by Linda W. Curtis

Illustrations by Wendy Bastings, Linda W. Curtis, Trinity Curtis.
Cover photo: Tracey Curtis Nielsen

Cover and Interior formatting by Rend Graphics
www.rendgraphics.com

Curtis, Linda W. 1939

Bench Therapy - Book One

ISBN-13: 978-0-9718065-4-2
ISBN-10: 0-9718065-4-3

Library of Congress pending

Bench Therapy

A Read-Aloud Book
Day and Bedtime

by Linda W. Curtis

Table of Contents

Table of Contents

Chapter 1
The Wrestler

Most folks avoid therapists because an office is so impersonal.

But Bench Therapy was appealing and the therapist went to the village hall to reserve a bench space in public spaces for an hour or two a day.

Although the appointment was made through the office, the actual meeting was at a designated park bench at a certain time. The therapist chose casual attire which made his clients feel more comfortable.

One bench faced the upper street across from a café and a bakery. If a client was agreeable, the therapist would suggest a treat and walk over, still talking as the charge was by the hour and eating with your mouth open was allowed.

The first client for Bench Therapy was a wrestling instructor at the local gym.

A competition was coming up and he was having fears about his competence.

The first donut was spent with him describing the sleepless nights, lying awake and feeling shame. The second donut brought out a confession of taking steroids to win in previous competitions. The third donut brought tears, and he tossed it into the trash can.

The therapist listened, nodding his head appropriately, and placed his hand on the wrestler's muscular arm affectionately. "What did you want to be as a kid?"

The wrestler's face brightened as he wiped his eyes. "Oh," he guffawed, "I wanted to be a cowboy, ride horses, go to races, you know."

"Did you have a horse?" the therapist asked.

"No, never could, no space for a stable."

"Well, here is my prescription." The therapist took out a pad and wrote the name of a horse stable that was currently hiring stable hands. "It's time to treat the child that is still within you."

A week passed, with no contact. But the second week, a phone call assured him he accepted a mornings-only job and was happy as a lark. The other stable hands were friendly and he had new social contacts. He paid his one-hour Bench Therapy charge with his new pay.

He also signed up for Bench Therapy Songs for next week. So, the therapist familiarized himself with western songs about riding horses.

Plus, he bought a pitch pipe. Hmm.

<<<< *Comments* <<<<<

_____

_____

_____

_____

_____

_____

_____

_____

_____

_____

_____

Chapter 2
Therapy Songs

The wrestler couldn't attend a Bench Therapy songs appointment the next weeks. Just as well.

Three bookings were called in and he met the first client on a lovely morning, birds singing, light clouds in the blue sky and a soft breeze.

Loliana was a former operetta singer. She developed a throat problem, had surgery, but the problem was alleviated, not solved. No more church choir either, so she stopped attending.

She felt melancholy and "under the weather" every day.

The therapist explained they would begin with some childhood songs she sang way back in time. "Oh, good," she said "This is what my mother sang at bedtime." Even though a bit croaky, the words were clear and the therapist clapped after, with a big smile.

"Alright then," he said, "what about your first heartbreak song?"

Now, he'd hit a nerve and her mouth quivered as she sang a raspy version. The therapist wiped a tear and said, "That was good, brought back my own memories."

"Let's get to something jaunty, like something you would have heard on The Muppet Show years ago."

Well, jaunty it was, and she stood up with a bit of bodily jive, so he stood up and made moves to match. Cars driving slowly down the street beeped their horns and some gave thumbs up out their window.

They both laughed and sat down on the bench. They sat in silence for a few minutes and then he said. "I'm going to write a prescription with the name of a nursery school that needs volunteer help for an hour one day a week teaching pitch pipe matching notes and some easy songs."

She took it and cocked her head. "Really? Well, I'll give it a try."

The next week, nothing.

The following week the voice on the phone was jaunty as she described the children's responses. She was given a small stipend, which she used on her therapist's charge, and signed up for the Bench Therapy Rhythm and Blues.

<<<< *Comments* <<<<<

_____

_____

_____

_____

_____

_____

_____

_____

_____

_____

_____

Chapter 3
Dockside

His first two appointments had left his office with the tissue box emptied as clients wept through their stories of neglect and afflictions. He had two chairs facing him in the office, one a plush cocoon-like, the other a straight back, not even padded. He would motion to which chair by the manner in which the clients entered, slumped and dejected looking or agitated.

He was anticipating the next day 11 a.m. bench therapy. This one at the marina dock bench, facing the sail boats tied up neatly in rows. He smelled his client before he saw him, a chef at an Italian restaurant. "Hello, Emilio," he said.

Emilio grumbled and snorted, "If you say so." With a pause, Emilio sat down and began a lament of being overworked and underpaid.

And surrounded by crabby co-workers.

"Why just last week..." he went on to share his regrettable employment, and the therapist almost dosed off with the warm sun on his face. He snapped back and said, "So how did you manage that?" Again, another doze and he knew he was food-deprived.

"Emilio, I brought a minced potato salad sandwich, and two sodas. Will you join me?"

"Really? Well, okay, I've not tried that." At first bite, his eyebrows flipped up, he made slathering sounds and said, "Wow, this is good."

"I'm writing you a prescription to attend the restaurant associations annual meeting featuring salad bars. I will only charge you half my fee if you will take your boss. That'll help pay the fee at the door. Emilio looked puzzled, thought a bit, then said sure, he'd at least try.

This was another client he would not hear from for a few weeks until he saw the restaurant ad in the newspaper about the new salad bar, with Emilio and the owner in Chef hats and smiling.

The wrestler turned stable-hand called in to cancel any future appointments, sent his appreciation and offered two tickets to attend next week's Derby races.

He read that Loliana and her nursery choir made the news, featured in the family section. The article said she'd received other offers and the parents of the children were so pleased.

She canceled her rhythm and blues bench therapy but he readied for that therapy anyway, pan lids for cymbals in a tote bag, as well as metal pans and large spoons and, just in case, two kazoos.

<<<< *Comments* <<<<<

_____

_____

_____

_____

_____

_____

_____

_____

_____

_____

Chapter 4
New Benches

The therapist enjoyed the change of scene so much he visited City Hall to find out where the new city benches were located. In explaining it to the receptionist, she asked about his hourly fee, and like all the other clients was taken aback gulping at the one-hour charge. Then, blowing a raspberry, said, "That's fair, considering the enormity of my problem."

So she showed him the bench behind city hall and set an appointment for the following week.

She was off work at 3 PM so they needn't worry about others having lunch together.

The therapist showed up in jogging clothes and brought a bag of candy for snacks.

She munched a bit and then said, "Is what I tell you confidential?"

"Of course, no one will ever know. Just start at the beginning."

It wasn't long before his hair began to prickle on his neck as she disclosed she'd discovered an inhouse embezzlement and she would likely take the blame.

"Do you know who it is?"

"No, not a clue."

"Is anyone driving a new car, bought a new house, or done something expensive?"

"I don't really know."

"Well then, here is my prescription." He pulled out his pad and wrote down the email of a hacker detective. "Do not use your name, use a code name and find out how much he will charge. Give the names and addresses of all you work with and send to this detective to peruse their bank accounts and large expenses. Next time we meet, I will have the info from him so you are out of the picture. In the meantime, I have a second prescription, this one to volunteer for the garden clubs decorating committee this week. Here's the name of the chairwoman who will be delighted to have you involved. It will take your mind off of the problem."

The next week behind the city hall, he had the information, so her next step would be to reveal it to the right person. The mayor's office was just down the hall so the paper he gave her was clean of fingerprints and she was to grasp it with tissue so she'd not leave any of her own as she placed it on his desk when he took a bathroom break.

Only a week later he read in the newspaper of an arrest of someone at city hall for an embezzlement, happily not his client. The therapist learned she'd joined the garden club and was pleased with new friends and projects.

<<<< Comments <<<<<

_____

_____

_____

_____

_____

_____

_____

_____

_____

_____

Chapter 5
Balcony Gardening

It was a blustery day and the therapist and his client both sat under umbrellas with dripping edges. "I like rainy days" said the client. "Really? " he responded, "What do you like about them?"

Wrong question as the long pause became uncomfortable. So he approached from a more pleasant angle. "Good for the flowers, you know," he said and added, "I have a small garden on my apartment balcony."

She turned her head to him, now interested. "And what do you raise?"

"As much as I can," he laughed, "veggies, flowers, I even raised a pumpkin last year."

"I live in a one room apartment and don't have a balcony. I'm too confined and feel so gloomy, especially around sundown."

"Ah," he said, "A lot of folks suffer from the sundown blues. In tribal days humans had an inner alarm clock of gloom at sundown and it meant to return to family and camp."

She turned her face at an angle, looked him in the face and said, "Can it be that simple?"

"Well," he said, "Here's your prescription. Find a different apartment with good morning sunlight and a balcony. Make it a quest, make a check list, see a realtor. Then attend one of the meetings of the Balcony Gardeners. Here's their website."

After their good byes, he watched her walk away, jauntier than the way they'd met.

"A quest, a vision, that's a cure," he whispered to himself, rain dripping from his Fedora hat.

He visited the Balcony Gardeners website and to his amazement a new member had organized a pumpkin contest. Guess who was handing out seed packets and smiling? His client.

Uh, oh, now he felt inspired, paid his membership dues and drove behind hardware stores to raid their dumpsters of empty buckets. On his balcony he assembled a high rise of buckets with spaces between for the leafy vines to grow outwards. Then, he too, bought a package of award-winning pumpkin seeds and grandiose sunflower seeds.

<<<< Comments <<<<<

_____

_____

_____

_____

_____

_____

_____

_____

_____

_____

Chapter 6
Porsche Therapy

This one hour was for the office, but when the huge man entered the office, he sat on the wooden chair. Whomp! The chair legs gave out and down he went onto the floor.

The therapist immediately went around his desk to help him up, but found he could not lift him.

"No, no," the big guy said, "Get me that stool, I'll use that for leverage."

With much grunting, the big guy was up and standing, seemingly okay.

"How would you like to go outside and sit on the bench outside the Café?" he asked.

"Good with me." was the answer and they took the elevator down.

On the bench, the therapist asked, was that your first chair bust?"

The big guy laughed, "Yep, but that's not my problem. My problem is I bought a new Porsche and got in okay, but couldn't get out and had to call 911.

The Emergency folks worked hard, ended up greasing the door edges and several hauled and others pushed from the other side. Since this was not a medical emergency or accident, my Med-Care would not pay and I had a whopper charge. I've been afraid to get in since."

"Hmmm," the therapist was amused, imagining that situation. "Were you alright?"

"Oh, I was bruised, but my ego was devastated. I've been eating non-stop to ease my humiliation."

"Well, food therapy works, if the conditions are right, but are the conditions right?"

"No, I'm a goodies-aholic. I hide snacks and treats all over my apartment, like the Easter bunny hides eggs. At the end of my day, I like to do the hunt and treat myself."

The therapist took out his note pad. Here's the prescription for two weeks, and then we'll have another bench therapy. You are to become a member of "Slim Now" that meets in this building twice a week. They'll load you with packaged low-calorie yummy goodies that you can hide. I think you'll be pleased.

The big guy took the prescription and smiled, as the cure did not remove his pleasure-treasure hunt. As he walked away the therapist smiled, too.

In two months the big guy could likely fit in the Porsche.

<<<< Comments <<<<<

_____

_____

_____

_____

_____

_____

_____

_____

_____

_____

Chapter 7
Song Therapy

Two weeks later, a slimmer man walked in the door, and buoyantly announced not only was the membership successful, he had learned new places to hide his stash, from the hems of curtains to removable floor wall boards.

The therapist accepted the check, and asked, "When will you try to get in the Porsche again?"

"Oh, I'm not even going to try. A used car dealer is also a member and has offered me a good trade in for a roomier sports car. A lady in the group has her eye on me, and I may need a courtship car, if you know what I mean," he said, winking at the therapist.

They chuckled as he opened the door and the big guy left.

Then in came a teary handkerchief wringing lady.

"My dear, he said, "Would you rather sit outside on a bench with me on this beautiful day? Here, take my arm."

Out they went and he sang all the way down the elevator and asked, "Do you sing much?"

"Oh, I used to, the whole family attended a gospel singing church. But that was long ago. "

"Did you have any favorites?"

"Oh sure." And she rattled off numerous songs, many Elvis recorded before his rock-n-roll fame.

Once on the bench, he would sing the first line of a song and she'd sing the next. At one point he began toe-tapping, and then clapping and they sang louder, laughing over their blunders.

"I have a prescription," he said taking out his note pad. "Try-outs for a gospel choir are this week In that theater down the block. I'm writing a letter of recommendation also as I know the choir director. Here's the time and show this at the door. "

He heard back quickly on this one. She was accepted, was given sheet music to practice.

And she paid her fee.

He attended the first Gospel production the next month and was delighted to hear her solo, brief, but enjoyable. He was singing to himself for weeks after.

<<<< *Comments* <<<<

_____

_____

_____

_____

_____

_____

_____

_____

_____

_____

Chapter 8
Illusion Therapy

He could barely hear the new client on the phone, it was almost a whisper. They set a time for the bench near the statue in the city hall grounds. She told him she'd wear a red hat, and pert it was, even had a feather.

"Well, hello," he said, "Now that's red!" She smiled, then carefully turned her head slowly this way and that carefully as though she was being watched.

"I'm a private detective," she said, "and I can't get over this feeling someone is watching me. I mean, I watch people all the time, I'm hired to do it, but this feeling won't leave me alone."

"Oh yes," he bluffed, "It's the "eyes everywhere" syndrome. Many people suffer from it, not just detectives."

"Is there a cure?" she asked.

He pulled out his note pad. "I'm writing you a prescription for changing your appearance so quickly and smoothly, that if you were being followed, you'd fool them. Here's the name of a thrift store that has wigs and hats, and reversible tote bags to carry them in. Buy a series of three and practice quick changes at home, and tell no one. Oh, and learn to do easy hair styles and braids."

She stood up, and said, "Let's walk behind those bushes." So they did and she took off her hat and stuffed it in her bag, and put on a scarf. Then she put on oversized sun glasses. "Like this?" she asked.

"Oh, yeah," he answered. "In one week, meet me in my office with your tote bags and show me how you've progressed." She meant business alright, because the next week she'd become a quick-change artist.

He didn't even recognize her at his office door. Within the first 15 minutes she made three costume, hair and glasses changes.

He applauded with amazement.

"And what about the feeling you are being watched?"

"Let-em watch! I feel so good about the ease of costume change, it's like a game."

"I can use this in my detective work, too. Thank you." She reached in her tote, that was in a different colored tote, that was in a different colored tote, and pulled out his fee.

"You are amazing!" he said.

"Yes, I know," she answered.

<<<< *Comments* <<<<<

_____

_____

_____

_____

_____

_____

_____

_____

_____

Chapter 9
The Pastor's Cure

An office meeting with a pastor in a clerical collar was unusual. Polite and cordial, he expressed humility at having an unsolvable problem.

After all, he tended to the problems of his flock, but none had his problem. He was about to retire after 30 years in his downtown parish. And he was apprehensive about the future, cold sweat in the night apprehensive. He was showing signs of aging, and had a faulty memory.

Here's your prescription, said the therapist taking out his pad and writing. You are to begin an inventory of every church in the city limits, beginning with a widening circle around your own. Attend both Sunday and evening services and keep a note book. Every week you will send me the who, what, when, where and how of each service and what you agreed or disagreed with. By week two, we can begin to formulate basic differences in each sermon, look for similarities as well. Also note the general disposition of the congregation as they leave to catch comments.

After six weeks, with six different churches of different denominations, he told the therapist he preferred bench therapy as the weather was so pleasant of late.

They met on the bench on the hillside overlooking their town, and many church spires were in view. "Well then," said the therapist, "What was the one concept in common?"

The pastor chuckled, "That's not too difficult. They believe in a God of their own conception.

Then the consequential question, "Why are there so many different churches and beliefs".

A pause, then he continued, "It's also history. Each church has a history of folks getting together in homes, then buildings, then a church. Churches are mostly inventions of a community, village or city, of many related folks and neighbors."

The therapist asked, "Why are there so many churches with off-shoots of other religions?"

"Oh, that's a result of 'church-politics' where folks disagree with the message, or the folks in the congregation can't get along. Yeah, it happens a lot. In fact, I've decided to retire and start my own church. Here's my fee, and thanks. I won't need you again." He rose, and left renewed.

<<<< *Comments* <<<<<

_____

_____

_____

_____

_____

_____

_____

_____

_____

Chapter 10
Dog Walk Therapy

The therapist noticed the ad in the paper.

Bench Church, bring your own chair. All Welcome.

So, he found his folding lounge chair and drove over on Sunday.

When he arrived, couples were bringing in benches and flowering potted plants.

An amazing spontaneous structuring of floor space near the front resulted in three semi-circles of benches and chairs.

The pastor immediately spotted him and came over to introduce him to others.

A bit of small talk followed and one person slipped him his business card and said, "Call me, please."

The service was enlightening, the music hand-clapping rhythms and all sang joyfully.

Monday morning, he called the business card number only to hear music, plaintiff and sad, followed by, "This is Lisa."

"Hello Lisa, you gave me your business card at the Bench Church yesterday. At which bench in town would you like to have a therapy talk? I have a 3 p.m. free today."

"The one at Sadler's Landing, where the old train depot was taken down. I'll see you there."

And surprised he was to see someone so colorful, a dashing hat, fly-away hair, and high heeled platform shoes. And it was a guy.

"I usually don't take trans-gender clients. Would you like a referral?"

"I'm not in need of that, crossed that line a long time ago. It's my dog."

"Uh, sorry I don't do animal-therapy either."

"Oh no, my dog is okay, its just, well, it's just,..he keeps biting me." The guy pulled up his sleeve and showed some awful gash marks and scars.

The therapist took out his prescription pad and said, here's what we can try for one week.

Your daily walk will stop at many more hydrants and mail boxes beyond your usual walk route. Wear walking shoes to go the distance. Next time we meet, show me your arms again.

The next time, the guy rolled up his arms and showed no new gashes from his pit bull.

"Good "he said, "this week go a new route, only increase the number of stops." Dog cured.

<<<< *Comments* <<<<<

_____

_____

_____

_____

_____

_____

_____

_____

_____

_____

Chapter 11
Discernible Stenches

Bench therapy was going well, but the temps were dropping and Halloween was coming on.

He was not surprised to have a farmer enter his office in bib overalls, smelling like the farm.

After cordial hellos, the farmer looked at the therapist and with red-rimmed eyes pleaded, "Please help me."

"What, exactly?" the therapist asked, knowing that folks in general reply indirectly.

"It's my wife, she doesn't love me anymore. She says I STINK!"

The barnyard aroma was quite evident and the therapist took one of his tissues from the box and blew loudly. "Are you aware of any smell? "He asked, not letting on it was pretty strong.

"No, none. I've been around animals all my life, even ran over a skunk once and didn't bother me to bury it."

"Aha," the therapist thought. A non-smeller with non-functioning nasal glands.

"Well, we'll just have to find out which aromas are stench-like to your wife. I'll have a list of 87 discernible stenches and you begin with the sweetest and work to the foulest.

He took out his pad an wrote a prescription. "Go to a florist and buy a few of the sweetest, most aromatic smelling flowers and give them to your wife. Do not tell her it's an experiment. Call in if there's any results from the first seven stenches. Are we in tune?"

"Yeah," said the farmer, looking puzzled, but willing.

The results were amazing, she bedded him the first day thinking the flowers were a romantic gift.

He returned to the florist every day he went into town thereafter and bought another aromatic bouquet.

The next time they met on the bench at the park at the end of town. "She liked all those aromas, so we still haven't found the stench." the farmer said. "But that's okay, I'm enjoying this, so what's next on the list of stenches?"

The therapist noticed he was dressed a bit less farm-ish and was smooth shaven. "We'll try some of the soap aromas next. Be sure to lather these on in the shower to get the full effect."

Well, the full effect was indeed effective. He reported his wife was "all over him" and they still hadn't found any too sweet or pungent aromas she was evasive to yet. He cancelled his next appointment and said he could handle this himself.

<<<< Comments <<<<<

_____
_____
_____
_____
_____
_____
_____
_____
_____
_____

Chapter 12
The Escapee

An office appointment began cordially, but as he readied himself to ask the first question, the door burst open and a wild appearing man flung himself on the floor and crawled past the therapists legs under his desk.

"Help me! Help me! The cops are after me and I'm not the robber!"

His client stood up just as the cops appeared at the door, looked around and said, "Lock the door and stay inside until further notice."

So he rose as well, and said, "We need to continue our session. We'll just let the poor fellow catch his breath, then we'll shift our attention to him. Okay?"

He pulled his chair around so he sat nearer. "You said over the phone you were a writer with writer's block?"

"Uh, yeah, I had a couple of good sellers but lately no new ideas." He could see the fellows feet shifting under the desk. "Can we forget me and help him?"

The therapist realized he was too distracted, so went around the desk with his best smiley face and said, "Come on out. The door is locked, not even the cops can get in."

Fingers appeared, then a hand. The therapist took his hand and helped him up and made introductions.

"I'll bet you have a story to share with us." He flipped his waste basket over and sat down, with an expectant face as the fellow sat in his chair.

He'd stopped puffing and shaking and told them of a misidentification and how he'd run up three flights of stairs to get away from being hand-cuffed.

"You haven't committed a crime so we are not aiding or abetting a criminal. I shall regard you as a client, and actually, you two may have something in common. So I'll be quiet and you two chat a bit and find out what."

Good thing, as they discovered he had dated his sister, went to the same high school and the sister worked in the financial building in the next block. "I'm picking Susilou up when I'm done here, want to tag along?"

A knock on the door and a voice, "All clear, they've caught the perp."

"Thanks," the therapist said, giving the fellow a fake mustache, and letting them out the door.

<<<< *Comments* <<<<<

_____

_____

_____

_____

_____

_____

_____

_____

_____

_____

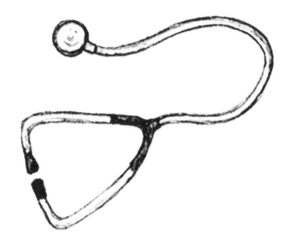

Chapter 13
The Doctor

Medical professionals were well read and sought literature rather than therapy. Yet, the doctor that called for an appointment was a small town doctor having a sense of failure of falling behind in helping his patients.

So the therapist asked if he'd like to spend his hour on a bench in his home town park.

That sounded good to the doctor as he was on call for some "iffy" patients and wanted to be near in case of an emergency.

The drive was an hour away, but a beautiful day for a drive. The park was down town and part of the town square. They shook hands and looked into each other's face, reading the lines.

"I hope you have an answer for me," the doctor said. "This hangs on me like a gray shawl, that I'm old, outdated, and can't do the watchful job I need to."

"Let's talk about you first, any hobbies?"

"Are you kidding? Who has time for hobbies?"

Just then, a skate boarder went by too fast, attempted a curve and flipped. Ow.

He was out cold, no movement, and doctor was on him in a flash. He checked his vitals while the therapist gazed at someone who was adept, who knew what to do and by the time the ambulance lifted the kid into the van, he'd called the nearby hospital to give them directions. The van sped away with revolving bright lights and sirens.

As the therapist sat down with the doctor he said, "No worries, there's no charge for time spent in emergencies. We can go longer or reschedule if you'd like."

The doctor looked up at the sky, watched some clouds, and said, "Let's keep on talking, and you can come with me to the old folks home, now called Golden Manor assisted living."

So they went to the Golden Manor and first to the welcome room for visitors. He was so busy greeting folks and introducing the therapist as "a friend" that the time slipped away.

"Just one minute," he said, "I must stop in to see the doctor whose place I took in private practice."

A white haired, bent over fellow, loudly said his name with joyful expectancy. "I hoped you'd come today. The current staff doctor is on leave and we need someone. Can you help us?"

Well, of course. To the therapist, he said he needed no more therapy as this was a clear solution. He could help the folks he had already cared for most of their lives. And his.

The therapist drove home, pondering the unexpected result, but then, weren't they all?

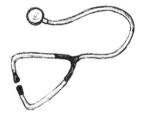

<<<< *Comments* <<<<<

_____

_____

_____

_____

_____

_____

_____

_____

_____

_____

Chapter 14
The Scientist's Lesson

The therapist decided one day to remain sitting on the bench after his session.

He smiled as he saw the person he helped walk away, leap, and click his heels.

While sitting, a young girls voice asked from behind, "May I sit here?"

"Of course. I have finished a therapy session and was just enjoying the day."

"Do you give advice?" she asked, slipping around the side, and slowly lowering herself.

"Well, no, we try not to. We encourage the person to discover their own direction. Do you feel you need advice rather than self discovery?"

The girl was frail, almost painfully thin. She was wearing a waitress apron. "I'm working myself through college because my parents refuse to help. They say a woman's job is in the home, not in college and certainly not as a scientist."

"Are you a scientist?"

"No, not yet, but I am taking science courses at the college and I'm working three jobs to pay for tuition and a room at the women's dorm. I'm getting B's and the scholarships are going to the A students. I've tried over and over and am just discouraged."

The therapist asked, "Have you heard of the law of compensating factors?"

"No," she said. "What is it? "

"It's for you to find out." He took out his prescription pad and wrote it down. Then he gave her his card and said to call with any results. He rose and walked away and did not look back. He had his umbrella that day and swung it in a jaunt as he walked.

At the end of that college semester, he did get a call with a message to meet. She was excited to explain she'd learned that any disadvantage has an advantage and any loss will also have a gain.

"I couldn't understand it at first, but then I was fired from my job and had more time to study. I was eating soda crackers and jelly and hot jello, instead of tea on weekends. I had a cafeteria weekday lunch ticket and I learned to make sandwiches for the week-end from loading my main meal. I volunteered to help the dorm house mother and she rewarded me with a resident job that paid part of my tuition. I was on call to help the young ladies with problems so I gave up my other jobs."

Is any smile so wonderful as the triumphant?

<<<< *Comments* <<<<<

_____

_____

_____

_____

_____

_____

_____

_____

_____

Chapter 15
The Dancers

The therapist noticed the limp right away.

"Did you have an accident?" He asked the well-dressed man.

"Oh, hah, don't I wish," he answered.

"No, but it's the root or foot of the problem. I'm a dancer and the woman I love is a klutz at dancing and no matter how many times we've practiced, I go home with sore toes. This last time, bones were broken and I am just now out of a foot cast."

"Hmmm, the therapist pondered. "What are your interests, besides dancing?

"By profession, I am the rare animal coordinator among the association of zoos, actually international."

"Really? And are any of those trainable, like dogs do tricks?"

"Actually, yes, we've recently rescued a southern Asian sloth and its has fingers, thumbs, frontal vision, and responds to music and can mimic."

The therapist took out his pad. "I'm writing you an unusual prescription, and it means research and finding a mate for your sloth. You will teach them to dance together, with treat rewards as dog training, and some simple sign language, too.

For yourself, find steel-tipped dancing shoes. Have your girlfriend find simple dancing music they respond to. Mind you, it may take many tunes before you find what makes them move in rhythm."

No news is often good news, and a full month passed before he heard from the dancer again.

Yes, a mate was found and shipped over. The sloths liked each other right away, even hugging with arms around each other. The music testing was daily, with more than a hundred different types of music, including primitive and tribal rhythms, and written up as a science thesis for the girlfriend who was finishing her degree in Music Therapy.

The Zoo was most helpful as the visitors were allowed in to view the study and the results were so cute that word of mouth brought in more visitors, including the press. The thesis was part video with the sloths dancing to "The old soft shoe." They were named Ginger and Fred.

Once the sloths and the couple rehearsed in unison, and swapping dance partners, the TV media recorded them. They even had specialty ballet-like shoes made for the sloths, with a hole on one side of each for the opposable thumb.

The dancer and his partner also improved now that his toes were protected, and he had fewer sore toes. They were accused of exploiting helpless animals by RARE, the Rare Animal Restoration Association, but the case thrown out of court since no animal was harmed and no financial gain to prove exploitation.

<<<< *Comments* <<<<<

_____

_____

_____

_____

_____

_____

_____

_____

_____

_____

_____

Chapter 16
The Laugher

"What a wonderful day, ha, ha, ha," the jokester remarked to the therapist as he met him at a bench outside a local theater.

"Indeed, it is, shall we stop in a that street vendor and get some snacks?"

"Oh,ha, ha, a good idea." So they each paid for a double dip cone.

Sitting back on the bench, the therapist asked, before the cone was devoured with loud slurping noises, "What's on your mind today?"

"It's me, I have a laughing disorder and really want a girlfriend, but they are all turned off by me, like I don't take them seriously."

This was a new one for the therapist who was quite clueless. The answer would have to come from outside sources, so he took his pad and wrote the name of a speech teacher for the theater acting class beginning this week.

Well, lucky strike or fate, the "ha ha guy" strode into his office the following week and said clearly "Ask me a question." He spoke his answer clearly, and one would never guess he had a disorder.

His story was remarkable.

He signed up for the class and had progress the first night in learning how to breath after speaking. His class mates had an assortment of speech impediments and wanted to become actors. Best of all, they paired up, and he had the "luck of the draw" - the cutest little ha ha gal to practice with each other.

"Better than that," he said with a smile, "We kinda liked each other and smooched a bit in the props room behind the curtain."

"Hmmm, I see," said the therapist. "You each have the same problem to solve but is it likely you can solve it in the same way?"

"Well, we both practice 'Rubber baby buggy bumpers' and others like 'Three Smart Fellas and they all felt smart,' and can now breath the last word to end abruptly without the ha ha's."

"This week's class we all show our progress out loud to the others. My partner and I are working on a duet speech, and hopefully can make it through this joke without laughing."

The two became a comedy team, joke telling and laughing or groaning with their audience.

<<<< *Comments* <<<<

_____

_____

_____

_____

_____

_____

_____

_____

_____

_____

_____

_____

Chapter 17
The Lepidopterist

On a sunny day on a hilltop bench, the therapist sat enjoying the scenery.

Trudging up the hill was a lone soul, stopping to rest a bit, then continuing on.

"A pleasant day, don't you think?" The therapist asked.

"Not if you've got this." The therapist gazed down on bulls-eye hornet stings on his neck, red and now rashy from the itching.

He didn't even speak, just looked at the poor soul with inquiring eyes.

Without hesitation, the soul answered, "I married a Lepidopterist."

A spontaneous utterance on his part, "Oh, no!" and regretted it immediately.

"I see you've had some experience" The therapist was obliged to tell his story so the poor soul would "spill the beans."

The therapist told him, "My girlfriend raised huge caterpillars in boxes under her bed. So when we married I had no idea how noisy all the munching of leaves was a night."

"Then you have some idea, a nuisance factor.

Now I have a large dog, but don't think that's even comparable. Now she's into artificial insemination of insects to get new hybrids, in particular, a honey produced by hybrid hornets, half bee. So I have the stings of the escapees."

He sighed and continued, "I'm a used car salesman, and people wince if they see hornet marks on my face and they go to another salesman. I promised I'd help Julene with her bee-hornet breeding for her graduate work in exchange for taking care of Backus, my dog, when I'm at work. But I can't take it anymore. Some loose hornets made a bag nest under the bed, and one night I was awakened by a loud buzzing, and they attacked!"

Hmmm, the therapist, thought as wrote on his prescription pad. It may be time to fight fire with fire. Stinger-to-stinger warfare. He told the stressed-out fellow, "Research everything you can on the species being bred. Bring your notes into my downtown office next week. And your aroma may be a clue to the hornet's hostility, so change your deodorant, toothpaste, and any other lotion for your work. When home, shower immediately with an aroma free shampoo."

The next week, though, was a dud. The situation was solved with her finishing her research, and put the last hornets in the freezer to perish. The therapist was paid with several large jars of honey, instead of check or credit card. He noticed the label. HHH. Hybrid Hornet Honey.

<<<< *Comments* <<<<

_____

_____

_____

_____

_____

_____

_____

_____

_____

_____

Chapter 18
The Birdhouse Snatcher

The therapist seldom had requests like this. The fella told him up front he did not need a therapist or anything issue-related, but hoped for insight instead.

He was a crafter and sold bird houses at craft fairs. Of late, his customers complained their new birdhouses were missing from their yard and bought another but were grumbly about the cost.

The therapist had dealt with compulsive thieves before, especially shop-lifters. But bird-houses? First of all, they'd need a ladder so must be fairly agile. They'd likely live in the area like a neighborhood kid. Profiling the perp was fun but the craft fella had no clue as to who.

So, the therapist had to tell him, "With no evidence of a recovered birdhouse yet, make sure you put identifying mark on the bottoms for the police, if recovered. A label just peels off."

No charge, just a hand shake and the fella walked away.

As the therapist sat on the bench, a van with the signage 'Charity Food Service' drove by with a bird house in the passenger window. How odd is that? He jotted the license and called his hacking friend to find it in the license bureau database. He promised him a bench lunch in exchange.

He drove to the county border and saw the van come out of a forested rut road and head back into town. The therapist waited a minute and then drove into the wooded road until it came to a field of tents and lean-tos around a cooking campfire.

So this was the homeless camp he had read about. He parked and walked a path around a hand pump, probably left from pioneer days. An old out-house, too, farther back in the woods.

A few kids were playing aside a small creek and a woman was rinsing out something. A group of men were putting something up in a something up in a tree, a birdhouse!

He immediately stopped, turned around and walked back to his car and saw more in the trees facing the camp. On his way back to his town he made an appointment with the crafter to meet him, and they'd go together to see if he recognized if any were his birdhouses. When he picked up the crafter the next day, he first walked inside the woodworking shop that smelled of pine, birch, fir, maple and willow. ahhhh.

All around on shelves were the most creatively designed birdhouse he had ever seen. He could barely tear himself away, but they had to know the truth. And they did. The birdhouses were the ones stolen from the crafters' customers. At first he thought of calling the police for an arrest, but then he remembered," Do onto others...." He hired the homeless and gave them tools and supplies and paid for new birdhouses. The therapist wept with compassion.

<<<< *Comments* <<<<<

_____

_____

_____

_____

_____

_____

_____

_____

_____

_____

_____

Chapter 19
The Cold Feet

Yes, the talk of the town, little Robbie Hansen was getting married this week-end.

The church congregation had watched Robbie through his years of Sunday School, then as a church usher, and were very happy when he and Sissilou announced their engagement at Thanksgiving by tinging his wine glass with a spoon, standing with a mega-smile.

That was then. This was now, on the bench with the therapist.

"Cold feet, I know it's called cold feet, but its more like a terrorized heart. What can I do to make it go away?"

The therapist reached for his prescription pad. "Do you have a grandmother too old to attend the wedding?"

"Yes, Grannilou, she lives an hour north, and cares for my Grampy."

The therapist handed him his phone. "Call her now, ask if you can come visit soon, before the wedding." The cold feeter asked, "And this will cure me?"

"Better than that" the therapist added, "You will find heart treasure."

They'd agreed to meet again two days later, this time on a bench facing west so they could see the sundown.

On the bench, with golden rays on their faces with sunglasses, and wide brimmed hats, they both sat for a while and just enjoyed the colorful clouds on the horizon.

"You were right," he said. "Grannilou said the cure for cold feet is a warm heart, but I must open the door to my heart with a song she taught me."

He sang it out loud, croaked out midway, but regained himself and finished a most beautiful love song the therapist hadn't heard in years. Seems Grannilou and Grampy sang that as their courtship song 60 years ago, and they sang it when times were rough to get through gray days.

"I've been singing songs to Sissilou on the phone and we are trying to pick one that the band can rehearse for the wedding dance at the reception.

"So you don't know what it is yet? " the therapist asked.

"We'll know it when we hear it," he said, rising, shaking hands, and striding off.

The sunset was beautiful.

<<<< *Comments* <<<<<

_____

_____

_____

_____

_____

_____

_____

_____

_____

_____

_____

Chapter 20
The Bookworm

Jeremy had so many books that he knew he needed help when he had marks on his face and body each morning from having slept on them in his bed after he fell asleep exhausted each night.

So, he asked the therapist what to do to on the bench by the river on the outskirts of town.

"How many do you have? " He asked attempt to discern the scope of the problem.

"Enough to start a library."

"Let's take a ride," the therapist told Jeremy. And so they traveled around the city stopping at small houses placed on the roadside. The small houses were all different, and all held books.

The therapist explained, "They are gift books as both keepers and lenders. Here's a sketch pad, make some drawings."

"I'll drop you back at the bench and write a prescription for you to construct one within this next week. Bring it back to me at this bench with some books next week and we'll mount it right here. I'll get a temporary permission from the town hall."

The excitement at Jeremy's work in the hardware store was noted by several employees who began their own book houses and shared lumber with each other.

Jeremy had no idea so many people hoarded small pieces of wood and their small house construction used up much of it. He began raiding the trash bins over at the lumber yard.

When Jeremy drove up, he had a yellow wooden book house, no windows and a hinged door one side. The therapist set the house on a post, standing back to admire.

"Now, we'll meet back here in one week, but here's your next prescription. It's a visit to a local wallpaper and paint store to get ideas for décor, like siding, stonework, even Victorian designs."

A week later, Jeremy brought a new friend. "I hope you don't mind," Jeremy said, "but I've enlisted some help with the signage. Meet Glorilou, a calligrapher who can letter free-hand on the house. See this?" He held up a panel with "If you love books, take one. Return or not."

As the therapist examined the beautiful lettering on a colorful background, Jeremy checked his book house on the post. It was loaded with hardbounds, paperbacks, mysteries, romance, even kid books, and he was so pleased he closed his eyes and looked faint.

A week later, he unloaded his books from a tote bag, looked grateful, and said gratefully, "The solution was in the circulation of generosity."

IF YOU
LOVE♡
BOOKS
TAKE
ONE...
RETURN
OR
NOT

LITTLE
LIBRARY

<<<< *Comments* <<<<<

_____

_____

_____

_____

_____

_____

_____

_____

_____

_____

Chapter 21
The Courtship Counselor

Talk about stress! His appointment with another counselor, this one for romantic reconciliations, had him unusually anxious. His insights had worked successfully so far but this one had "a damp rag smell" and as she explained what had gone wrong in the last three consultations, he wondered what else he could offer.

He knew to treat her disappointment and never sympathize. "Here's your prescription," he said, jotting in his pad. "First, find a new place for consultations. Several wedding chapels in the area allowed couples to visit to see if compatible with the numbers of their expected guests. These were empty between weddings and had lovely benches and landscape views. Second, be sure the couple looked out at a tranquil scene, not the parking lot. Third, always bring a food and drink in a picnic basket so that they munched as they talked. Fourth, give an empty journal to record their courtship memories."

A week later, the counselor was smiling. Yes, a couple had made up after their session and another expected this week. One of the chapel managers was interested in her business and took her card. Seems more couples needed their help then they knew.

Not just for couples in trouble, but as a service to make the preparations more enjoyable, including relaxation techniques.

She showed the therapist some breathing and stretching exercises, then gave him a neck massage so relaxing he almost fell off the bench.

She thanked and said she had found her way. As she rose, he felt a pang of time passage, another success but another goodbye.

He sat for a long time before eyeing the fast food shop down the road. Time to move on and he walked to the small outdoor patio tables where several folks were already enjoying the food.

And, lucky him, he saw one of his former clients who invited him to join him. Not only did he get all the news, he received praise for his bench therapy and was told he was recommended to others. They laughed, shook hands, and left an unusually nice tip.

Back in the third-floor downtown office, he realized how droll it was. He went online and found large wallpaper panels of scenic views of the Atlantic coast, sailboats, seabirds, fresh clouds. He chose the one that felt the most refreshing and ordered it. In fact, he wrote himself a prescription to do so.

<<<< *Comments* <<<<<

_____

_____

_____

_____

_____

_____

_____

_____

_____

_____

Chapter 22
The Splinter

Benches are not all alike. The newer ones are in the town, but once into the County Parks, the repair is less and the wood has splinters. All old wooden benches and tables are suspect.

And so it was that day, his appointment was in the County Riverside Park overlooking the river below. His new acquaintance was on crutches and took a good deal of time to make it from the parking lot to the first bench.

The lament was short and to the point. Since his car accident, his loss of job, and moving in with his parents, he was having trouble adjusting back to his family life, especially his father who thought him a "Nair-do-well."

Now the therapist knew he should not provide social services advice, so relied on the fellow's lifestyle to give a clue. "What is your main interest in life?" he asked.

"Oh, everything baseball. Try to watch all the games, and now, until my leg is better, I can.

It's just that my Dad expects me to pay rent to cover the food I eat, and I do a lot of snacking."

A rumble of thunder in the west said get to shelter, now. In the nick of time, too.

They ran toward the baseball field's shelter, a team was also running. It poured and poured. Finally the fella stood up and crutch-walked over to the team manager who had contacted all parents to come get their kids early.

The therapist watched him. He saw he was a charming personable kind of guy as the managers responded to his chat. He also saw, the manager give him card with address. Then, with a large smile, he crutch-walked back and said, "I may have a job."

They sat at one of the wooden tables. "Here's my prescription. The rain has let up and the kids are all being picked up now. So, take this. You are to read the local newspaper and find the school's sports history, so if you are interviewed you'll be knowledgeable."

As he slid over to hand it to him, he screeched an ow, held his backside, after having jamming himself on a large splinter. The manager recognized his problem, offering help with a red-cross kit he always kept handy.

"You'll have to drop your drawers if I'm to tweeze it out. Gather around guys and face out so no one can see what's up."

"Drop your drawers," the manager said. He tweezed out the splinter, raised it up in the air for all to see, then handed it to the therapist as though a gift or souvenir. The gain would be the new job. But the pain was, well, in the butt.

NO
PAIN...

NO
GAIN!

<<<< *Comments* <<<<<

_____

_____

_____

_____

_____

_____

_____

_____

_____

_____

Chapter 23
The Loser

Gambling was an addiction few could break, and his next case, well, he might not be able to help him. Once the brain is fixated on a behavior or substance, it tended to hold fast, unless...

There it was, the big "unless."

"Do you have other pursuits than horse and dog races?" the therapist asked.

Yes, I volunteer once a week at the animal shelter.

"Doing what"

"Oh, whatever, from cleaning cages to taking the dogs out on a leash for a run. But I don't think I'll continue, there's just too much sadness."

"What's the problem? "

"Same old story, too many animals, too many bills."

The therapist now did something he had never done before. He remembered his college statistics course and the law of probability. What if... what if his loosing streak had run out?

He wrote a prescription to meet with a professional gambler he knew who could give him info.

"Take notes and bring them back to the bench near the railway next week."

The therapist read people's body posture and generally knew who was having an uplift and who wasn't. This one was unusual as his clothing was different and he was dressed for success. His stride was different as he approached the bench, but remained standing. Where did this new confidence come from?

"I met with the guy you recommended who invited me to his gamblers club. It's a group of men who diversify and gamble with shared winnings, so even losers still have a gain."

"So the object is to win money to share the results?" The therapist wanted to be sure.

"Yes, and the sharing isn't just for ourselves, we each contribute to a charity of choice."

"I guess I know which one that is for you."

"You are so right, the animal shelter. And some of the other guys want to help, too."

"And my fee," he asked, "Was this earned from last night's get-together?" "You bet!" he answered.

<<<< *Comments* <<<<<

_____

_____

_____

_____

_____

_____

_____

_____

_____

_____

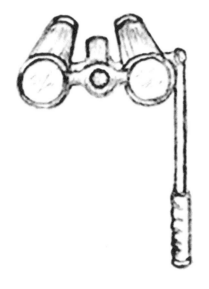

Chapter 24
Ms Incog Nito

A fine day, he arrived at the office early only to find a strange stranger waiting outside the door.

"Come on in," he spoke, welcoming to her.

He went right to his desk, that faced the door, and said, "May I have your first name?"

"Incog, that's spelled I N C O G." Unusual, he thought. "And your last?"

"Nito, spelled N I T O."

Realizing he had been spoofed, he dropped his pen with a grand gesture and said, "Alright, what is your given name?"

"Theodora, Theodora Roosevelt."

He picked up his pen and asked, "Are you sure?"

"Yes, and you can call me Teddy for short."

He dropped his pen again, swung his chair around to the big window, shook his head and asked, "How may I help you, Teddy?" and tried not to snicker.

"I'm being followed, probably a fan, and it's making me nervous. I'm performing at the Hazelton Theater tonight and would like you to sit in a chair facing the audience and later tell me what you sense. Here's two tickets." Up she rose and out the door before he could confirm he could attend or not.

"Well!" he said Jack Benny style. "I'd better call a forensic lab worker friend and invite him but explaining they will not sit together."

"I presume someone in the audience will reveal a facial expression or some posture that indicates they are a threat. Bring your opera glasses that have the hidden camera.

I'll have mine on my lapel. I'll give you an ear phone and a wrist watch to speak into so we'll be in touch." Surveillance was so much fun sometimes.

The audience was jovial, and when the curtain pulled, a cheer rose as Teddy was perched on a water fountain, jiving to a boomateeboomboom song.

He scanned the audience and saw the perp right away. So did his friend. They came from each side and helped him by arm grips and he said, "We have a prize for you, come this way."

Out front they handed him to the security guard and said, "You might want to talk to this guy."

The next time Ms. Teddy came in, she paid her fee and said she was not followed all week.

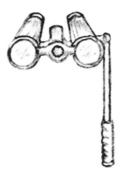

<<<< *Comments* <<<<<

_____

_____

_____

_____

_____

_____

_____

_____

_____

_____

Chapter 25
The Pie Cure

He certainly understood the anxiety of the lady on the bench. She had been in a foreign country doing missionary work and her recent blood test showed a rare monkey disease for which there was no cure.

He took out his prescription pad and wrote: "Eat a slice of a different fruit or nut pie, everyday in a different place for one week or until your next blood test. Keep me informed."

She took the prescription and read it over and over and finally asked, "Are you sure?"

"I have great confidence in the pie cure," he said, "It is, after all, something, not nothing."

She had to acknowledge that as a fact and so began her search and her favorite pie: pecan.

All week she'd smile at the waitress or waiter and say "Can I hear your pie list?"

It rang like music to her ears, and she ate eighteen different pie slices until her next blood test.

The result? You guessed it. Those little microbes were not able to withstand the curative powers of pie. The doctor declared her either cured or in remission.

Which, of course, meant she'd need to continue her pie therapy.

The therapist only heard back once, with the fee paid, but also a drawn image of a smiling face and an alphabetical list of pies she'd consumed.

Apple, dutch and plain, banana cream, blackberry, blueberry, boysenberry, cherry, coconut cream, cranberry-apple, mincemeat-raisin, mulberry, peach, pecan, pineapple, pumpkin, rhubarb, strawberry-rhubarb and raspberry.

The therapist went down to the café in his building, and asked, "What kind of pie do you have?"

<<<< *Comments* <<<<<

_____

_____

_____

_____

_____

_____

_____

_____

_____

_____

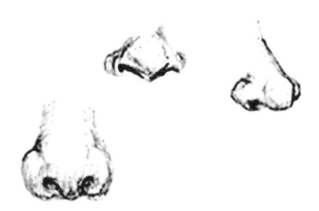

Chapter 26
The Droodler

Oh, this was a puzzler, with feelings of malaise for no reason. He had no interest in his career as an office worker taking and filling book orders, no future, no goals. They sat on the bench and made small talk about the birds that were flitting by from the mulberry tree, loaded and ready to drop thousands of berries.

"How do you fill your time?" the therapist asked.

"I droodle, silly little drawings about anything." he answered.

"Are you an illustrator?"

"Oh, heavens, no. I took a drawing course once and the instructor red-lettered every one with 'Line quality not consistent.' I was one of those kids with poor penmanship in school and my practice pages never made the bulletin board. Never."

The therapist smiled, and remembered his penmanship received poor grades. He took out his note pad and wrote this prescription.

"At work, at home, have a small sketch pad, inconspicuous and easy to use. Cartoon your fellow workers, without them knowing it. Practice noses first, then profiles, then full head."

He added out loud, "The next week, postures and poses, standing first, slumps included. Funny is good.

Come back in two weeks with your sketch pad, which we will now call your cartoon pad, as line quality is preferred inconsistent."

The fellow left the bench rather jauntily, and since he was off work for the day, bee-lined home to find his previous droodles and organize them.

When he showed up to the bench two weeks later, he had much more than a sketch pad, he had a bulging case of drawings to show the therapist. And laugh, noses were definitely funny.

The therapist asked if he could have the pack of cartoon droodles to choose some for the newspaper family page that asked for their readers to contribute.

"Sure, why not. Put any caption you want with them. Maybe I'll think of some myself while working on postures and poses." The therapist said goodbye and added, "Oh yes, you get A+".

And there it was, in the Sunday paper's family page. A picture of three noses in a row and a caption that read: "Guess which of these is a cowboy, an opera singer, or a musician?"

There was no right answer, but it lead to family discussions and laughter, which is one on the goals of newspapers, not just reporting the daily dilemmas.

Is there any joy as great as seeing your achievement as an A+ and in the local newspaper? The cartoon was such a hit the editor asked for more and even gave a small stipend for usage, and the therapist's fee was also paid.

<<<< *Comments* <<<<<

_____

_____

_____

_____

_____

_____

_____

_____

_____

_____

Chapter 27
The Egg Thieves

"Are you sure?" the therapist asked the chicken farmer.

"Positive. And I know when they are sneaking in because our dogs bark but by the time I get dressed and out to the coops, they're gone."

"Hmm. Chicken egg theft therapy to ease the pain. Did you tell the police?"

"Of course. Not one of their deputies is willing to sit out all night waiting for the thieves to show up. It's a petty theft. They didn't even take fingerprints."

The therapist's eyes squinted, his eyebrows furrowed and said, "I'm going to loan you my battery powered motion detector camera. You can watch the coop and when motion is detected, it turns a light on and you hear a bing and get an image on your computer."

So, he took it, set it up, and went to bed. BING. 10:30 PM. He had only been in bed a short time after turning off the lights of the house. Someone must have been waiting for him to go to bed.

Oh, this was so planned. And there they were, kids, a boy and a girl. A soon as the light went on they ran towards the woods down the road.

The next day, he walked down the road to see who got on the school bus. There they were, but he didn't know what to do, so made another appointment with the therapist.

After rolling his eyes several times thinking, he said, "Let's look at the homes on that school bus route. I'll go online and get the property owner from taxes. What's the number on the mailbox?"

What he found was a rental cottage down by Sulter's marsh. He looked up the owner's phone and called, a real estate firm. He carefully inquired about the renters and found a single mom and two children lived there, about to be evicted for lack of payment.

The chicken farmer, a bachelor, listened intently and wrote down their names. He returned the camera and thanked him, paid his fee and was gone.

That was it? The therapist felt deflated. So, he did more digging and found the chicken farmer was a widower of one year. The therapist drove to the home of the two children and introduced himself to the mother. He said his friend needed help at his farm, if she was interested in housekeeping, and if the children could do chores.

You know where this is going. The answer was yes, yes, and yes. The rest becomes history with a wedding in the spring. But you knew that, didn't you?

<<<< *Comments* <<<<<

_____

_____

_____

_____

_____

_____

_____

_____

_____

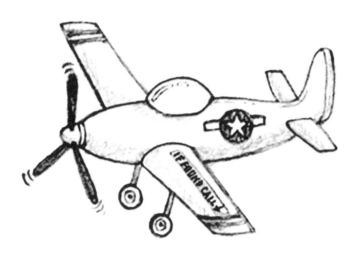

Chapter 28
The Poor Soul

The bench therapy was a bit chilly that day so they moved into a fast food shop and took a booth, of course, booth therapy.

They shared a sub and sipped sodas as the poor soul lamented "Humans were so crazy. Every day the television is full of crap news, dirt, and destruction."

The therapist took out his note pad and wrote this prescription: "Do not read a newspaper or watch television for one week. Instead, look for the most cheerful magazine you can find and read an article a day for one week." Handing it to the poor soul, he added, "Let's eat here again, same time next week so you can give me seven article summaries."

The enthusiasm the next week was obvious and the poor soul ordered a whole sub sandwich for himself and talked with his mouth full.

Now, the therapist was a good listener, asking provocative questions, and even took notes, he just couldn't watch.

He learned the poor soul had no social life and was interested in model airplanes. The following week was the air show contest for home-made craft, and his prescription was to go, chat up the craft makers and bring back a report with photos.

The photos were great and he'd asked for some autographs. He learned about a flier's club of small craft, several divisions based on different modes of propulsion. He was reading more and not watching television at all except for some reruns of the Dukes of Hazard.

The third week he announced he did not need therapy any more, paid his fee plus brought in a small model airplane. They went outside to the bench and watched as the poor soul wound up the rubber band propelled propeller and released it. Zoom, it flew high into the air, got caught in an updraft and was last seen flying over the woodlands towards the lake.

He'd had the good sense to etch in his name and phone number on the model, and sure enough he got a call from a lady who said it flew into her patio and crashed. He drove over to pick it up only to find she had repaired it and gave it a new tail wing. Her garage was a dream workshop and they met again, and again.

The therapist knew he'd never see his client again, but that was okay, they were happy.

<<<< Comments <<<<<

_____

_____

_____

_____

_____

_____

_____

_____

_____

_____

_____

Chapter 29
The Chain Link Fence

Oh no, awake all night by barking dogs, the eye bags and red rimmed eyes told the therapist this guy was really weary. He said, "I've called the police, the neighbor, and now you. What am I going to do?

"Easy," he said, "you must move. But first, tell me about yourself."

"Well, I'm quiet, I like solitude, don't go out much except for art shows"

"Are you an artist?"

"Hah, no, I wish. I'd like to take more courses, but the college is too far away and my job in the opposite direction."

The note pad came out and he wrote the prescription with the name of a realtor to find a place nearer the college and enroll right away, as the semester was about to begin.

EUREKA! Not only did the right abode become available, and cheaper, but he found two art night courses. His move was simple and quick, only two trailer loads and he was in.

The end of the semester meant the student work went on display and a judging with a prize of free tuition the next semester. The therapist received an invitation and off he went.

Eighteen weeks later he drove to the college. He knew some of the art faculty and chatted some up and carefully asked about his client as the works were numbered without names.

He was astounded. One large canvas was of three large dogs behind a chain link fence, all apparently barking. Another of a guy dancing with a large spotted dog, the dog's feet on his shoulders. The third painting was himself dancing with a large dog.

None of the hilarious paintings earned an award, but the therapist didn't care. He called his client and congratulated him and offered to buy the dog-rider painting.

"Oh, sorry," he answered. "I already sold it and the others the night of the college art display. But you can see it down at the local museum, second floor, the director thought the dog-rider bore a resemblance to his brother."

The therapist shook his head, thanked him, and asked about his general health.

"This is the finest I've ever been. The future is so bright now, thank you."

<<<< Comments <<<<<

_____

_____

_____

_____

_____

_____

_____

_____

_____

_____

Chapter 30
Joke Therapy

Wiping her eyes, she wept all the way in and sat in the therapist's chair by mistake.

The therapist sat in the client's chair and waited until she caught her breath and could speak, even though between sobs.

It was a sad story. A tornado had wiped out an entire suburb in a southern county. He'd read about it in the newspaper and wondered how they would cope.

"It isn't just the house and the car, those can be replaced. It's all the photos and family treasures are gone, gone, blown away."

Feeling a bit weepy himself, he said, "I'm going to give you a prescription to tell a joke a day in exchange for another joke, so you always have a new one handy. But they must be one heard from a family member already passed over. In seven days return with those jokes and who told them and write them down."

"Really, that's it?" She asked, cocking her head sideways, inquisitively.

"Absolutely! Even people in hospitals with third degree burns benefited."

On her way out the door the therapist asked, "Have you heard the rumor about butter? Well, I can't tell you, you might spread it."

A guffaw and she slapped his arm. "That's awful!" she said.

"I know," he replied, "but it worked."

"I've got to tell my sister" she said waving goodbye. "See you at the bench next week".

And what a meeting that was. She told of the nightly bonfires of scrap wood in her neighborhood, and folks sitting around.

One week after the tornado, the initial shock was wearing off and she stood in the glow of the flames and said in a loud voice. "Everybody, listen up. I am being treated for post-tornado trauma and part of the cure is a joke a day, told by a passed family person. In a few minutes, after you talk among yourselves, please volunteer to tell their joke."

The sound of chatter and laughing was music to her ears and spirit. One tall fellow stood up and said, "A snail crossing the road was run over by a turtle. Later, in the hospital, his friends asked what happened and he said, 'I don't know, it happened so fast.'"

After their groans and chuckles, another stood up, and another. She wrote them all down.

"If no-one minds, I want to send these to the local newspaper. The reporter has been coming out every day to see our progress and he should know we are recovering." Heads nodded.

<<<< *Comments* <<<<<

_____

_____

_____

_____

_____

_____

_____

_____

_____

Chapter 31
Lament Therapy

The therapist read about the jokes in the newspaper but little about the person. An insertion by the editor was especially encouraging. He asked, since so many had lost family photos and memorabilia in the tornado, for those who remembered or had photos, to send any information to the newspaper and they'd print it for the families and neighbors to enjoy.

The turn-out was unbelievable. The town spinster revealed her first kiss with her joke! The daily news increased sales and the editor was pleased.

Only one person signed up for bench therapy that week, and it was the oldest person in town. He was in his late nineties and had a good memory but had the old age lament, no future.

"Okay, Leon, this prescription is for daytime only, when you are at your best, no nights. Stay on your walker and visit the local VETS. You are to remember any stories shared and tell me next week. I know your hand is too shaky to write well, so I'll take notes and give you back a printed copy."

Leon's neighbor was a VET and when he heard about the Lament Therapy, offered to pick him up and be with him through the meeting. He even introduced him as their new doorman and greeter and that was in World War I with his grandad.

Many of the VETS were interested in his stories of his grandfather during their social hour and asked that he come again.

He was happy to do so, having inherited a diary of his Grandpa who served with several fellas who also had VET grandfathers. Some were victims of the recent post-tornado trauma and eager to tell family stories and also take notes.

In two weeks he was cured of his laments and busy on the VET's chapter's computer.

He shook his wobbly hand with the therapist, and shared that he was to be on a truck flatbed in the upcoming Memorial Day Parade with a sign that said, "We also honor children and grandchildren of VETS."

The parade was the best ever. The tornado-stricken neighborhood was in recovery and their jokes of former friends and family members printed into archival history. The local historic society took special interests, found school photos, and put up displays in store windows.

The therapist had never dreamed anything so simple could have such results.

We also honor children and grandchildren of VETS

<<<< *Comments* <<<<<

_____

_____

_____

_____

_____

_____

_____

_____

_____

_____

_____

Chapter 32
The Gag Reflex

"I don't know if I can help you." the therapist said to the caller.

"Your compulsive gag reflex seems more of a medical problem."

"I've already tried," the caller whined, "Please at least hear me out. I'll pay the full hour fee."

The therapist reluctantly said yes, and to meet at the bench in a wildlife park, a mini zoo where a animals were called by name.

"So," he asked as they sat on the bench and gazed, "have you always had this malady?"

"Oh yes, even as a child my grade school teachers kept an empty waste basket by my desk in case I let fly."

"What triggers you?"

Yicky stuff of any kind. Even people walking their dogs."

"Sometimes a cure is to increase the triggers, which then minimizes their impact."

The therapist took out his pad.

"See that gentleman over there with the rake and trash basket? He's in charge of the volunteers and they begin by cleaning the animal cages."

"I'm writing you a prescription to apply for a volunteer position. Keep a gag bag with you, and try to minimize your retching sounds by singing Old Man River or another bellowing melody. Practice at night till the wretch is covered by your vocal note."

"Okay, I'll try. I'll only do it a week though, and let's meet back here. But, no cure, no fee?"

"Sounds good to me," the therapist said.

The therapist dreaded the next meeting. His rent was due and he needed the money.

He sincerely hoped his "overdose of a bad thing" would result in a cure.

The first few days were horrific, but day by day the gagger had less and less reaction and he even suggested clean-up improvements so the volunteers sang clean-up songs as they worked. He paid his fee a week later and they both were pleased.

<<<< *Comments* <<<<<

_____

_____

_____

_____

_____

_____

_____

_____

_____

_____

_____

Chapter 33
Compulsive Collecting

"I can't see out my windows at home," the husband complained. My wife buys more and more plants, divides or does cuttings on the ones we do have. They're everywhere. I have to take them out of the shower stall if I want to use it. She even drives a convertible with plants in the back seat."

"That's an unusual compulsion alright. What about you, do you save or hoard anything?

"Just my book collection," he said. I have original signed copies of..." and he spent several minutes giving a long list of book names and their authors.

"How do you store them?"

"Floor to ceiling book shelves, every room and down the stairwell, too."

"Do you have any wall room for photos and pictures?"

"A couple. Why do you ask?"

"Because that is your starting point. Here's my prescription: Take down the photos and pictures and put them on the doors, use special hangers or tape. Buy grow lights and build new ceiling to floor plant shelves, as high as you can reach to water them. Choose just the window-hog plants to go on the shelf."

The next week he reported the shelving was built and the grow lights installed. The window-hog plants were positioned so he could see out the windows.

"And next," he mentioned, "I bought extra boards and built extra book shelving on the backs of doors, and removed the photos and pictures on both sides. The books were heavy, but I put wheels under the lowest shelf to ease door opening."

The therapist was pleased at his ingenuity and said so, and the fee was paid with good spirits.

"However, he said, eventually you will run out of space. What will you do then?"

"Oh, we've discussed that. We are due for an addition to our garage, with a greenhouse, too. I've bought a new chop-saw and think we can do most of the finish work ourselves. The garage addition will be ceiling to floor shelving, too. You can't have too many books, you know."

The therapist rolled his eyes and thought about the roll-away book storage under his bed.

< <

Chapter 34
The Malaise

No doubt, the therapist thought, this is going to be a mind-blower. Anyone this intelligent should have uplifting thoughts, intelligent uplifting thoughts.

He asked, "What gives you a feeling of fun?"

A long pause as the lady professor thought. That was a clue to a workaholic personality.

"Let me rephrase that, what do you think would be fun?"

Another long pause.

The therapist was attending a party later and sensed a need for an event, and to have fun watching other people having fun. So, he asked politely, "Would you accompany me to a party, a nice meal, and maybe some games and for sure dancing with a band? It's just down the block in the hotel conference room."

The lady professor smiled. "How lovely," she said, "I could use a break during this exam week.'

They walked arm in arm, strode in a similar gait, and he felt enlightened.

At the door they were met and given stick-on name labels, and her name was "Florise."

A charming name, meaning lady of the flowers. Person after person commented on her name.

And soon she was swept away to meet others. He stood and watched as they chatted and he realized she was "working the room." She moved again to another group with introductions and he joined her, asking, "What are you doing?"

"Having fun." she answered. "I love looking into the faces I meet. Aren't you having fun?"

"Actually, I'm watching you as your therapist."

"Well then, how about the first dance?" The band had settled in and the first notes almost raised their hair up. The beat nearly propelled them to move any which way and she began with an arm swinging torso bending movement that sent his posture into motion as well. They laughed as all around them joined in and made "woo woo woo" sounds.

After several dances, they moved to the buffet table and loaded their plates and sat with others, introducing themselves. Another college professor was there and he chatted her up, and exchanged business cards.

As they said goodbye she said, "Send me your bill. This therapy really worked!"

<<<< Comments <<<<<

_____

_____

_____

_____

_____

_____

_____

_____

_____

_____

Chapter 35
Tooty, Not Hooty

When Tooty came to the office for the first visit, she stood and carefully observed the walls, the ceiling, the floor, then to the windows and looked out to the view.

The therapist asked, "What do you see?"

"Your office is on the third floor, this part is only ten by twelve feet, ten foot ceiling, window view is east over the park, the structure is from the 1930's and has been refurbished at least twice. But that's just the suppressed architect in me. I'm really here to ask for advice, and I know you don't give advice, but hope you will consider some as person to person."

"All right, let's hear it, then. Do you want to go out to a bench, or to the café with a booth?"

"All of the above. Let's start here. I have met a great guy, and I am in the mating time of my life and think this is it, my true love. I've met his family once and they abhor me as they are upper crust financially and I'm an up-north small-town gal. I did not use the correct silverware at their dinner and other improper behaviors, like laughing at my own jokes."

"Hmm, and you want to change who you are?" he asked?

"Oh, no, I like who I am, polite, kind, well educated. I don't want to be 'Hooty-tooty.' But I must figure out a way not to embarrass my honey-man, or cause a breach between them."

"Let's head-on-down to the café, I'm buying," the therapist said, took her arm and smiled at the cute lady in her late twenties. She stood up and smiled back, took his arm and they sauntered to the elevator.

In the café, Tooty ordered pie, and he succumbed and ordered pie as well. As they forked pieces and tasted each savory bite, he finally said, "I doubt there is a solution. The more you try to appease the parents, the less they will think of you. You are who you are. If they make fun of you, turn it into humor. Make it into a song. Tell me a joke or story about yourself and we can laugh together."

They did and went out the café door laughing to the bench that overlooked the park.

He said, "Class distinctions have been around as long as civilization. They should not define you, at least not in today's world. As an educated woman you should strengthen what is good about yourself, and let the family get-togethers just be polite meetings. Disregard the long nose sniffing, the corner of the mouth smirking, the head tossing. Just be yourself. Maybe not telling jokes is the best advice I can give. If your honey-man loves you, he won't care."

"You are right," she said, "In an unsolvable situation, just strengthen yourself." She hugged him briefly and walked away, looking back once with a smile and a nod.

<<<< Comments <<<<<

Chapter 36
The Song Writer

"I've lost it, just lost it!" he said, referring to his inability to write new songs.

The therapist asked, "What kind of songs did you write?"

"All kinds, even songs for commercials, like the one on PaPa Burgers ad."

He sang it loud and clear and so the therapist joined him, both laughing at the non-harmony.

"Now there's a new fish burger that needs a tune, and the sponsor is paying big bucks for the right tune."

The therapist took out his note pad and wrote a prescription to research medieval minstrel songs and come back in a week with new words in the old tunes.

Did it work? Oh, my, did it. He brought in a small keyboard and set it on the therapists desk.

"Listen to this." He sang as he played.

"What fish is this, on my plate tonight," to the tune of Greensleeves and ended with "at PaPas tonight."

The therapist liked it but wanted to hear the others. One by one they extolled the flavor, that rhymes with ..... and the taste that rhymes with.... leaving the therapist uncertain which was the one most likely to be chosen.

"When's the deadline for entries?" he asked.

"Tomorrow, and I'll drive it down in person. I won't know for a week or more." the song writer replied.

"In the meantime," the therapist said writing his prescription, "you should write a joyful lyric and this time choose war tunes."

Did it work? Oh yeah. He sang new words in an off-beat rhythm to "When Johnny comes marching home again, hoorah, hoorah."

The therapist liked it, tapped his foot, clapped his hands.

The new words to the marching tune of "Those Cassions Keep Rolling Along" was really a muscle-jerker. Again, off-rhythm syncopation made it new.

"I'm cured," he said. "I can harvest old tunes and replant afresh with new words."

The therapist smiled, but regretting seeing him leave, the office now seemed so empty.

<<<< *Comments* <<<<<

_____

_____

_____

_____

_____

_____

_____

_____

_____

Chapter 37
The Thrill Seeker

"It's no use," he told the therapist. "I've had every thrill a man could have. I've taken my motorcycle everywhere in the States, and even rode standing up on my cycle on Thrill Hill in Florida."

The bench was facing east and the morning sunrise golden and glowing. He went on, enjoying his elaboration. "I've done sky diving, underwater cave swimming, and even walked the rim of a red hot volcano. I'm not married so I'm free to have solo adventures."

"Wow, that is impressive," the therapist said. "Any injuries?"

"I always had proper gear. I'm only crazy, not stupid." he answered.

"I thought that was the other way around," the therapist jested with a smile. "I have a prescription for you," he said taking out his notebook. "You will spend one week at Emma's Day Care as an assistant. They'll clue you in."

"Will it help?" He asked dubiously.

"See me in one week at Caton's horse farm off the main road at sundown. There's a bench and a picnic table, so bring some food, if you'd like."

The next week, a very agitated man stepped out of his car. "How could you do that to me?"

"I'm anxious to hear how it went. Don't spare the details," he said placing a bag of Donuts Delights on the picnic table.

The Thrill Seeker couldn't speak at first.

"I had no idea taking care of little kids could be so scary. I was attacked by a two year old, smeared with food feeding a one year old, and some were not potty-trained and I was taught how to change a diaper. Yick."

He made a face and tweaked his nose between his fingers. "I had to play with the little boys and teach them to share. Then I had tea parties with the little girls and sat on a little chair and sipped from a tiny cup. When a baby in one of the four cribs started crying, I had to pick them up and lullaby them in a rocking chair. By the end of the day I was so fatigued I went right to my apartment, took a shower. One time I found mashed potatoes behind my ear. I literally fell into bed each night."

"Then, I was told to learn sign language to help a cute little four year old deaf boy play better with the other children. I ended up teaching a whole group of four year old's sign-language, and they taught the three year olds. It was the best part of the week."

The therapist asked, "If you weren't a bachelor and had children of your own, would it have been easier?"

"Oh," he paused, rolled his eyes up to look at the sunset, pursed his lips and said, "I get it now. Dads have so much to do in their lives, they wouldn't be seeking thrills." Then he added, "I think I'll propose this week."

The therapist smiled at this revelation.

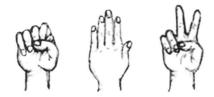

<<<< *Comments* <<<<<

_____

_____

_____

_____

_____

_____

_____

_____

_____

_____

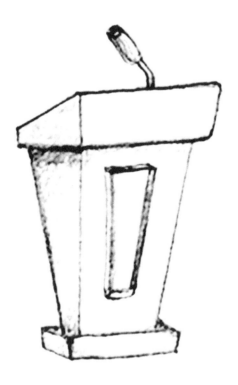

Chapter 38
The Whiner

How he got into office is anybody's guess, because to talk with him was just plain irritating.

He sought bench therapy to help him as a politician to better talk with voters. They met at the bridge bench atop the highest point over the river and he had to walk holding onto the rail to get there.

After greeting each other, the whiner began by complaining about his colleagues who more or less pressured him to get help. The therapist saw the problem - first, attitude, second speech rehearsal.

Fortunately, the therapist knew the speech instructor at the local college and wrote a prescription for him to take Speech 101, entering midway in the semester with some tutoring to catch up. The one-on-one mentoring made his new speech pattern effective.

The attitude adjustment would take an entirely different course, and for that he made an appointment with the warden at the county jail to meet with volunteer prisoners and take notes. He was told to not speak much, except for asking questions. He was to listen, not talk.

Questions he could ask included: What are you in for? Were you fairly represented? If a prisoner would whine, he could likely hear his own tone.

The therapist met with the whiner at the Smorgasborg Café the next week for booth therapy as the bench was soaked on the rainy day.

But something better happened. He combined what he learned from listening to the prisoners with his speech class instruction and he was scheduled to give a public address for his party next week. As he spoke, his tone was different, definitely not whining. In fact, he had also improved his posture for his performance as a public servant, ready to listen and make politician's promises.

The therapist could hardly wait. He did write a prescription for a better suit, shirt, and tie.

They practiced his walk to the podium. Then they practiced the steady eye sweep of the crowd, and slight but distinct smile. His arm motions were also appropriate, but he was told he should grip the podium if he needed to. Last, he practiced how to pause and take a deep breath before continuing.

The day of the public speech, the therapist was in the audience and listened and watched intently, "Way to go!" he said. The person next to him asked, "Are you related or something?"

He laughed and said, "Am I that obvious?"

The person said, "You should learn poise, like our speaker. He's a natural."

Of course, insult aside, he knew his job was done.

<<<< *Comments* <<<<<

_____

_____

_____

_____

_____

_____

_____

_____

_____

_____

Chapter 39
The Listener

The therapist smiled when he heard, "When I was a little kid, my mother said to go outside and tell a tree my problems. And I did. That stayed with me and I still lay it out to a favorite tree. It's just that there's no feed-back. I don't know if it really heard me or not. How do I find out?"

"It's probably more than the tree can absorb," the therapist answered. "Good thing you found bench therapy."

"I'll say. I am a woodcarving artist and want to enter this year's competition at the fairgrounds. My problem is, no inspiration. All the others have grand sculptures and nothing is lighting up in my mind."

"No worries, mate." the therapist said joyfully. "You've already told me something that may be helpful. Here's a prescription for you to draw thirty-two ears, all different and bring back your sketches next week, same bench, same time."

And, as prescribed, the woodcarver came with the sketches, all different and well done. The therapist had bought a battery operated wood carving tool set and gave it to the artist.

"Do you know Steinhoffer's Woods, behind the city park? I've arranged with the owner for you to carve an ear on several trees facing the park, so if anyone looks over the fence, they'll see the trees appear to be listening. They're not to be more than twelve inches tall, as the bark must be removed in a patch for the carving, then sealed after so bugs don't get in."

"Really? Can't I use my own woodcarving tools?"

"Oh, of course, this is for fine details. You could use a little wood burning set to put on your name as well."

One week later he had only six done, but he explained that prototypes always take longer than the last, and best, finished project. And, he added, he had a junk yard pile out back of rejected prototypes. A light bulb lit up in the therapist's mind.

"Here's your next prescription. You are to select the best rejected wood pieces or logs, and add ears and garden decor. You need not pay me this week and instead sign up for a craft's sale table at the county fair and pay that fee."

Well, the results were fantastic! The artist created not only ears, but chins, noses and frown lines. Some were paint or stain enhanced, and his name as artist etched on each one. HE SOLD OUT! People bought his carvings as art décor for their patio and gardens.

<<<< *Comments* <<<<<

_____

_____

_____

_____

_____

_____

_____

_____

_____

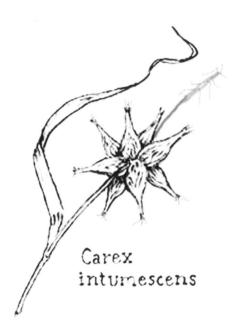

Carex
intumescens

Chapter 40
The Sedger

Sedgers, like birders, are generally nice people. While the birders are looking up, the sedgers are looking down and finger combing what look like grass clumps.

"So what's the problem?" the therapist asked the sedger.

"Well, the birders make a life list of all the bird species they've seen, many more than a hundred," the sedger explained.

"Several years ago I began my life list for a sedge genus named *Carex* and already have seen forty-seven species and listed them in my notebook. The problem is, sedging has become compulsive, and some of the species are in parks that close at sunset or private lands. I would need a permit or permission, which I don't have, to collect seed heads and leaves to identify them."

"Well," the therapist said, thinking out loud. "I know birders have binoculars and identify birds by sight and sound. How do you identify sedges like Carex?"

"Magnifying glass or microscope. The little parts are mostly less than a quarter of an inch and our eyes can't see to such tiny details. So I dress like a KamaKazi with dark hood and gloves and sneak in from the side roads at night. I can pull the plant I've seen during the day out of the soil and put in my plastic bag to take home."

"Is it safe?" the therapist asked. "No, not at all. I crawled into some animal nests, almost died of a heart attack by a raccoon attack, and last week I stepped into carnage, a carcass, and had to shower for hours to get the stench off me. I want to stop my compulsion for sneaky collecting."

The therapist took out his pad and wrote that he should prepare a speech about his collection so far, scan and enlarge his images and present it to a local Friends of the Park Club. He was to ask the president of the Friends to set a date at the park office conference room. He gave him the name of a ranger who made presentations for help in set-up.

Well, as nervous as he was, he found the park's Friends interested in his *Carex* collection since *Carex* was one of the largest and most under-reported species.

Afterward, he took the group out for a walk looking for *Carex* and found ten species within ten minutes. The Friends newsletter gave a good report with photos and his scanned images.

Uh, oh, sedge fever had begun and more people inquired if he could do it again. The Park authorities gave him permission to collect as long as he pressed and mounted the specimens on herbarium paper for their own office staff to learn to identify them. He kept the duplicates for himself and by the following week his bench therapy had a joyous report that he now had sixty-four of the state's known eighty species.

The therapist, too, caught sedge fever, compulsive sedge collecting, and began his life list.

Carex
inturnescens

<<<< *Comments* <<<<<

_____

_____

_____

_____

_____

_____

_____

_____

_____

_____

Chapter 41
The Competition

"No, I didn't know," the therapist told the old coot in the chair.

"The only reason I went to Beach Therapy was for curiosity. I heard the lady therapist was a looker and she charged ten dollars a minute for you to ask a question and get an answer. Most guys were out in ten minutes. I didn't have a question so I just asked how she liked being a therapist and were there any difficulties."

The therapist was shocked and appalled to realize he had competition. He took three slow deep breaths, then asked with squinted eyes. "What were the difficulties?"

"Oh, some guys wanted a date afterward. Some just wanted to tell their bizarre experiences. She listened, told them what she thought, hit the timer on the clock and said that'll be one hundred dollars at ten minutes whether they were done talking or not."

"Where is this beach therapist located?" he asked.

"Down by the old marina, next to the hot dog vendor, the ice cream snack shack, and the popcorn stand."

"I'm closing for the day," he told the coot. "Call in and set another appointment," he said, grabbing his hat and fast out the door.

He knew exactly where that part of the park beach was as one of the benches he used for therapy was on the bluff above.

Right away, he knew that was her tent, even before he saw the sign. "Therapy ten dollars a minute. An answer guaranteed."

Two gents were ahead of him, so he chatted them up. "You guys having therapy today?" he asked.

One responded, "I sure hope I get some useful advice. My daughter ran off with a used-car salesman. How awful is that?"

The other one said, "You think that's bad? My daughter ran off with...." and he stopped, choked up and waved, no more talk.

Out of the tent stepped a young man in his twenties. He said over his shoulder, "Thank you, I never knew that."

In went the next fellow, and they heard almost all of his lament, he talked so loudly. They could not hear the answer, just the clock binging that ten minutes was up. He seemed determined as he stepped out and past them, rolling up his sleeves.

His turn, uh oh. He recognized her as one of his former clients, but didn't let on. She had gone blonde, or was wearing a wig, he couldn't tell. She had suffered a heart ache but moved on.

"Speak your problem, sir, and I will answer right away to fill our ten minutes," she said, showing signs of tiredness, not even looking up.

Quickly he made up a story of how he was fired again and again at jobs because he couldn't keep his hands off the ladies.

"Easy," she said. "Always wear gloves and never get close. Back up, turn around, walk away. If they find you aloof, so be it." The clock binged, she stood up, took her sign down and left with his hundred-dollar bill.

He watched her walk up the slope to the parking lot and drive away and felt relieved. His was true therapy, and not advice-giving like her beach therapy, a con, while his therapy was an art, however amorphic but effective with often unanticipated and joyful results.

<<<< *Comments* <<<<

_____

_____

_____

Chapter 42
Snake Hair

While snakes do not have hair, in this case, the hair had snakes.

The therapist was a bit startled by the fuzzy-haired young lady with fake snakes curled into her hair, one protruding to the side over her ear.

"Wow," he said, motioning her to sit on the bench beside him. "I'll bet you have an interesting story."

"You bet!" she said with some defiance. "There's nothing in the Constitution about hair styles, and nothing in the school rules either about hair décor. I want to wear my snake hair for graduation and everyone, and I mean EVERYONE is against it."

The therapist was speechless at first and waited, even whistled a bit, then took out his pen and pad and wrote a prescription:

"At graduation, you'll wear a cap. When the orders are taken for cap size, in addition to your robe size, choose a larger cap, one you can conceal your hair style under with nothing hanging out. At least for the diploma part. Your family will be pleased, and so will the principle. At the very end of the ceremony, graduates take off their caps and throw them in the air. That will be your finest moment."

And so it happened. To her surprise, several other students decided to do the same with other ornaments. So when caps came off, parents gasped at fake frogs, bugs and spiders.

Others laughed, so happy it wasn't their child. Grandparents just shook their heads. One student had shaved his head, and the crowd turned to look at the shocked parents who gasped loudly.

Naturally the hair décor at graduation went before the graduation committee to prevent any such antics the following year, but then handed it over to the PTA, that did nothing.

The therapist had attended the graduation to study the reactions. The relative humor was well received by this community and all was okay.

<<<< Comments <<<<<

_____

_____

_____

_____

_____

_____

_____

_____

_____

_____

Chapter 43
Gratitude Therapy

The day was perfect for bench therapy, a light breeze, sweet air fragrance, light fluffy clouds floating in a deep blue sky. "Ah," the therapist thought. "How could anything ruin this day?"

That's when the unhappiest man on the planet sat down beside him and said, "Do not ask how am I. It's too dismal."

"What have you to be dismal about?" the therapist asked.

The answer was blurted out, "Everything!" He stood up and waved his arms. "I want OFF this blankety-blank planet!"

"Tell me about yourself," he said pleasantly, deliberately unreactive.

The guy paced around the bench and snorted. "I work all day, I work into the night. I have no fun, all I do is work, work, work."

"What do you do?" The therapist realized the guy was venting anger and would let him continue to vent. He was right, after several more rants he sat back down on the bench.

"I'm a veterinarian's assistant. My father is the vet and I've been his assistant forever."

"Ah, so it's not only the hours but clean-ups, and help with the surgeries too?" the therapist asked.

"You betcha. It's worse than that. My father is crabby all the time especially when I'm squeamish, like just this week, we removed a hemorrhoid from a mama duck so she could sit on her eggs.'"

The therapist took out his pad and wrote this prescription:

"Leave your current profession as soon as your father can find a new assistant. Expect bad feelings for a while as you may be kicked out. Consult a counselor at the local college and begin right away in the best course available, even if you are not 100% sure it's the right next step. Ask a friend if you can live-in for a while."

He did. His father was furious, but found a new assistant within the week. The next week on the bench the guy looked "wrung-out" but said right away, "You were so right, I needed to find my own life. And I've begun courses at the college and they had a job list board and I found a nice part-time job with nice people. I feel better and even had some good laughs with new friends."

Hmm, new job, new friends, new interests, this was directional. "Have you heard of Gratitude Therapy?" The therapist asked, pulling out his pad and writing.

"No, what's that?"

"'Every night before you sleep, think of three things you are grateful for, and say them out loud."

'Really? That's a prescription?"

"Yes," he answered, "and you could be one of the happiest people on the planet."

Was he right? Oh, yeah, because the next week he practically bounded into the bench and said, "This is my last therapy. Life couldn't be better. My father let me know he was sorry and said he understood. I got B+ and A's in my first college tests and started tutoring others, for pay."

He paused a bit sheepishly and said, "I called my Dad and the new assistant is really good with the animals. He even put a bandage on mama duck."

The therapist smiled, and said, "Let's walk up to that ice-cream vendor and celebrate."

<<<< Comments <<<<<

_____

_____

_____

Chapter 44
The One-Man Band

"Well, I am pleased to meet you," the therapist told the musician who had just sat down on the bench. "I sing your songs, a lot, especially while shaving in the morning."

"That's good to hear, thanks," the long-haired mustached musician replied. "But, it's come to an end. One by one my band has lost our members and now, I am the last one. I have songs to sing, and no accompaniment other than my own steel guitar. I can't retire from my life as a musician, and I have no other interests."

The therapist knew the solution was in the multiplication of his talents, a one-man band.

He took out his pad and wrote: "Go to Ernie's Inventions, a little shop off main street. He's got kazoos, foot drums, harmonicas. You name it, he's got it. Ernie was a guitarist once himself, 'til he had an accident rock climbing. Ask him for attachments to the guitar, and drums and cymbals controlled by your feet."

The next week, the musician brought his steel guitar that was loaded with additions, even a harmonica on a support bar at lip level. Behind him in a red wagon he pulled two drums with mechanical drumsticks and cymbals.

He explained he and Ernie had worked all week on a one-man song with his own backup.

True, the snare drum attached to a lever on his left foot was not the same as a "wipe-out" drummer, but it kept the beat and could swing over to the cymbals. "Would you like me to demonstrate?" he said setting down the drums and slipping his shoe into the strap connected to the drum sticks.

"Absolutely!" the therapist said and leaned back into the bench. The musician had a little stool he sat on and faced him. His voice was a cross between Willie Nelson and Buddy Holly through a kazoo.

The first bursts were loud enough without amplification and a crowd assembled and listened, and clapped. He then asked the crowd to join him in a well-known tune, and they did. One couple danced. A reporter from the local newspaper came by, stopped to listen, then took photos and sure enough, it made the next day's paper.

The next week, he returned without the instruments, and happily reported that he and inventor Ernie has added more, and he wrote new lyrics to old tunes using many new attached gismos. He paid his therapy fee with money he had already made in two gigs.

He'd placed an ad in the paper as a one-man band for parties and ceremonies and received a wonderful response, and he filled in his calendar spaces with engagement dates.

He shaved his mustache and braided his hair and had the drum lettered with his new band name: Johnny's No-good One Man band. He became locally famous.

<<<< Comments <<<<<

_____

_____

_____

_____

_____

_____

_____

_____

_____

FAMILY
PHOTO
ALBUM

Chapter 45
The Triplets

Can three ladies fit comfortably on a park bench? Yes, but the therapist wouldn't fit, so they chose booth therapy instead at the café.

"Well, ladies," the therapist said. "This is unusual for me, so let's do birth order and let the first-born speak first." The ladies were named, Jay, Jill, and Jane, and Jane spoke first.

"We have a problem with our professions, all different, demanding, and we don't get to visit each other except on holidays."

Second oldest, Jill spoke next. "Yes, our professions are different, but we hope to work together on some things, and socialize that way."

Jay, the youngest, said, "I'm a painter, have my own gallery shop in the mall outside of town. Jill is an auto mechanic and works at Steve's Garage, near here. And Jane, well, she's our politician and is running for mayor."

The therapist drew upon the forces of insightful thought and took out his pad and wrote: "Each of you will take a half day off and work along each one of your sisters at their work. Make a schedule and stick to it. Write a summary of what your sister's work is like and bring it back here next week, same time."

The ladies looked at the therapist as though he was crazy, but nodded their heads and said goodbye. The therapist needed those summaries to help with his next prescription.

The next week, he couldn't tell them apart facially, so he looked at their hands. Jill had blackened finger nails as a mechanic. Jay, the artist, had colorful paint under her nails. And Jane had professionally manicured nails as you'd guess, also.

They were asked to read their summaries aloud. The reactions were rather amusing and the therapist felt he was on the right track.

"Alright then," he said taking out his prescription pad. "This week, you'll take your camera and make no less than seven photos of each sister's work, but don't show them to each other until our next week's meeting."

The next week was exciting as each had eight by ten inch photos to show and explain. The love and caring each had for each other was revealed in their comments about the photos, and their responses afterward.

"Ladies, the therapist said, "You have performed admirably, both summaries and photos. Now, the time slots you made in your work schedules to visit your sister's work is now your home-made treasure.

You will set aside that time every week to meet at a new cafe midway between yourselves.

Bring the summaries and photos and work them into a family album that is to become a family legacy."

"Your fee is for one person, for three therapy sessions, as I think of you as a similar group."

They each gladly paid their share and left laughing and chatting about where to meet. He sat in the booth alone and watched, smiling.

<<<< *Comments* <<<<<

_____

_____

_____

_____

_____

_____

Chapter 46
The Exposer

The therapist sat on the bench a long time and wondered if this was a no-show. He had seemed agitated on the phone, almost desperate and he made room in his schedule to accommodate this late hour, nearly sun down.

Then after a whish and screeching brakes, a bicyclist came to a halt and dropped the bike.

"Sorry to be late," he said, taking off his helmet, "but I was being followed and had to take some short-cuts to get here."

"Followed by whom?" the therapist asked.

"Spies. They want the script to my next book because it has secrets no one knows, yet. This book will tell the truth, even if it hurts."

"You are in a precarious situation with an expose. Is it safe?" the therapist asked, needing to know if he was also at risk.

"Yes, safe enough until it's published. I don't know if I should leak the info to a reporter, or not, pre-publication. I hope you can give me an honest opinion of whether to go ahead or not. The person I'm writing about is in the news today for being blackmailed because she embezzled funds from a charity."

"I read that story," the therapist said. "Her statement was she borrowed it and planned to pay it back."

"Hah!" the biker retorted." She rolled me for a few hundred bucks as a donation, and I can't bear anyone using my hard-earned money as a donation for themselves."

The therapist was sympathetic and said, "Although you've done your research, I don't think you have found out enough truths to publish yet. I'm sending you to a detective friend of mine who can give you help in finding paper money trails."

Out came the prescription pad and the therapist wrote the name of the detective. "I'll meet you here next week, same time. Bring the info."

The next week, the fellow walked to the bench, looked confident.

"Oh boy," he said, "You were right. I only knew part of the donation pilfering. What I found, thanks to the detective's directions, is other persons were involved, and part of a larger donation fraud. Turns out, the detective you sent me to has a connection with other investigators in town, and they share information."

"He called me and said someone else was investigating and had enough info to publish, and I didn't, so I decided to lay low and see what happens. So, I won't be coming again, just know I appreciate you sending me in the right direction." He laid out his fee, shook his hand and walked away.

The therapist thought, there's a moral to this story, but he just didn't know what.

<<<< *Comments* <<<<<

_____

_____

_____

_____

_____

_____

_____

_____

_____

_____

Chapter 47
The Loner

As they sat on the bench, storm clouds rolled in, so they walked up the slope and under an awning of a hardware store with a bench.

"Who is your best friend?" the therapist asked.

"I don't have one, I don't have any," he said dejected.

The rain started and they watched the first big splats, then splatters.

"What have you tried?" the therapist asked.

"Well, I've gone to several churches, and they all want me to join because they need ushers. I tried ushering at one, but not any were my age to be friends with."

"Hmmm," mused the therapist, pulling out his prescription pad. "Go to the library and visit several sections, including the children's and young adult section. Take out as many as you can carry, bring a box if necessary, then find out which ones you would look at or read again more than once. Meet me at that bench again."

At that moment a rip appeared in the awning and both were dumped on. They both ran, but in a different directions, for shelter.

The next week was exciting because he brought some of the books and explained why he enjoyed them.

The therapist listened to the tone of his voice and said, "Okay, what I am hearing is you liked the children's books into young adult the most, and you really liked several non-fiction books with illustrations. Am I right?" He nodded a yes.

"I can't write you a prescription yet, but go back and do it again with new selections. Meet me here and we'll have a solution."

Oh boy! Oh, joy! The guy trotted off with his books and the uplift was enjoyable. But the therapist's work was just beginning. He went to the library and found all the reading clubs there and in the surrounding towns in the library district. He jotted down the meeting times and dates and included them in his next prescription.

To his surprise, the lonely guy had already found one from a poster on the exit bulletin board. The therapist said to try at least three of the seven reading clubs and report back.

He said, "If you don't think there is a potential friend in the first three, try the next. Next week is no fee, just give me your written results."

His response came in a letter in the mail, explaining he was moving to the next town with the most enjoyable reading club. He wrote to cancel any more therapy. He thanked the therapist and drew a smiley face of them both.

"I wonder if I should write a book," he mused to himself.

<<<< *Comments* <<<<<

_____

_____

_____

_____

_____

_____

_____

_____

_____

_____

Chapter 48
The Sundown Blues

The therapist had heard of the biorhythm dread emotion to return home before dark and heard it called the Sundown Blues before. Only this was an extreme case.

He asked, "How have you tried to manage it?"

"Oh, brighter lights has helped but I need more. After a day of work I'm too tired to go out for any frivolity. I need something else."

"Well, then." said the therapist, taking out his prescription pad.

"First, list the colors of all the walls where you live and plan to change them one by one. Go to the paint stores and look at the wallpaper books as well. When you return to this bench next week, bring some color samples. Only look at them under bright lights, you were right on with that solution."

The next week she brought some interesting new colors, not seen in paints before. She met an interior designer who invited her to look at some model home she had chosen décor for as well as wall color. She took photos on her cell phone and showed them to the therapist.

"So many choices," she said. "I could even have a Western room with a herd of horses in a large mural wallpaper on the impact wall, the one you see first when entering. Always a wow."

She went on and on with such enthusiasm their time dwindled and he suggested a donut treat at the Café as he took out his prescription pad.

She was to put in more intense lights in each room for the sundown hours. Back to the hardware store and find what was available.

The next week he was shown photos of the results, and each room was a colorful delight. She roller-painted each day after work, so she was busy every day of the week. She thanked him for this direction and paid this last fee. As they said good-bye, she turned and said, "Do you know anything about the new do-it-yourself flooring?

He smiled, new flooring could be addictive.

"Do you have a chop saw?" he asked.

<<<< *Comments* <<<<<

_____

_____

_____

_____

_____

_____

_____

_____

_____

_____

About the Author
Linda W. Curtis

Linda W. Curtis is a research
botanist who has written four
science books and many articles
for science journals. Now she
has written her first fiction
book, *Bench Therapy*, with forty-
eight laugh-out- loud or at least
chuckle-out-loud stories to be
read as daytime or bedtime
stories. Linda hopes the readers
will give significant eye-rolling

and eyebrow wiggles while reading the stories. A laugh shared
is one of the treasures of life, along with good desserts.

https://udayton.edu/blogs/erma/2023/12/bathtub_coin_collector.php
https://udayton.edu/blogs/erma/2020/02/manatee-sneeze.php
https://udayton.edu/blogs/erma/2019/12/santas-key-west-wreck.php
https://udayton.edu/blogs/erma/2023/11/the_last_sleep_out.php
https://udayton.edu/blogs/erma/2019/10/the-turkey-blessing.php

Made in the USA
Middletown, DE
22 January 2024